First American Edition 2016
Kane Miller, A Division of EDC Publishing

Text copyright © 2015 Chris Morphew, Rowan McAuley and David Harding
Illustration and design copyright © 2015 Hardie Grant Egmont
First published in Australia by Hardie Grant Egmont 2015

For information contact:
Kane Miller, A Division of EDC Publishing
P.O. Box 470663
Tulsa, OK 74147-0663
www.kanemiller.com
www.edcpub.com
www.usbornebooksandmore.com

Library of Congress Control Number: 2015954255

Printed and bound in the United States of America
1 2 3 4 5 6 7 8 9 10

ISBN: 978-1-61067-501-7

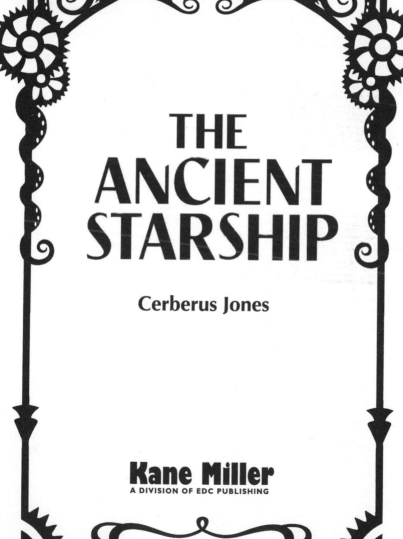

THE
ANCIENT
STARSHIP

Cerberus Jones

Kane Miller
A DIVISION OF EDC PUBLISHING

CHAPTER ONE

Amelia and Charlie panted as they ran. There had been some kind of crisis at the hotel that morning – the phone had been ringing and ringing long before dawn, and between each call, Dad and Mum kept having this hurried, whispered discussion. By the time the sun was up, it felt like everyone had been awake for hours. In fact, when Charlie's mum, Mary, had looked at the clock and screeched, "You're twenty minutes late!" Amelia was surprised it wasn't already lunchtime.

So here they were, sweaty and winded and still

half a block from school.

As they got closer, though, Amelia realized that there might be some sort of crisis at school, too. Thudding along the sidewalk, swinging around the signpost and racing down the driveway into the school, Amelia heard kids shouting at one another. Not just the usual loud, playful shouts, but angry yells. The school bell rang on and on, but no one paid any attention.

She glanced at Charlie, but he looked as confused as she was.

Slowing to a jog, they passed the school buildings and reached the playground at the back. Kids were swarming under the old crab apple tree.

"It'll be the start of World War III!" yelled Callan, a panicked look on his face.

"No it won't!" Erik snapped. "Don't you know anything? It's the start of a new world order – a new world peace!"

"What on earth ..." Charlie murmured, his eyes moving from one kid to the other. He found any sort of chaos very cheering.

Ms. Slaviero was in the middle of the playground, the old brass bell in one hand, but she'd given up using it. With her other hand, she put two fingers in her mouth and whistled.

For an instant, the playground was silent. The arguing kids stood frozen, stunned and staring at one another before turning to face their teacher.

"What is all the noise about?" Ms. Slaviero asked. "I could hear you from inside the supply closet!"

The quiet broke abruptly as six or eight kids shouted their explanations at Ms. Slaviero over the top of everyone else. She held up her hands.

"Stop, stop, stop! One at a time, please." She waited until they were all quiet again. "Right. Thank you. Now, Sophie T. How did this begin?"

"Oh, miss! Not her –" Erik blurted out.

Ms. Slaviero held up a hand again and looked steadily at Sophie T.

"Well," Sophie T. said, "it all started because of the aliens."

Amelia and Charlie glanced at one another.

"I beg your pardon," said Ms. Slaviero.

"Because of the aliens they found in Egypt," said Sophie T.

Amelia let out a breath she hadn't even known she was holding. *In Egypt – phew. Nothing to do with the gateway, then. Nothing to do with me or my family at all.*

Ms. Slaviero laughed. "Ooo-kay. Aliens in Egypt. I've got to say, I haven't heard that one before."

"It's true!" said Erik. "It was on the news and everything."

Charlie grinned at Amelia. "No way!" he whispered.

"Are you sure it was the news, Erik?" said Ms. Slaviero. "And not one of those funny Internet videos?"

"It was on the radio, too," said Callan.

"It's a hoax!" Sophie T. scoffed. "You guys are so gullible."

"It's not a hoax," said Callan, eyes widening. "It's a conspiracy. My brother told me all about it!"

"If that was true, we'd be blown to bits already!" Erik shot back. "They've come in peace."

"It's an invasion!" Callan shouted. "It's been going on for centuries. Wake up and learn the facts before it's too late, you drone! The whole world has been run by a secret society of giant space lizards since 1776."

Amelia gasped aloud. It was surely just a coincidence, wasn't it? Callan couldn't possibly know that the first alien Amelia and Charlie had ever seen going through the gateway under Tom's cottage had in fact been a giant space reptile. She hadn't told anyone about it. She shot a sideways glance at Charlie, but he seemed as bewildered by Callan's announcement as she was.

Ms. Slaviero turned and noticed Amelia and Charlie had arrived.

"Hello, you two," she said. "Well, if we've got the whole class here, I think I know what we're studying today."

Callan nodded fiercely. "The real history of the Illuminati and their plans to enslave all humanity."

"Er, no ..." said Ms. Slaviero.

"How proof of alien existence will unite all humanity in a new era of peace and enlightenment," said Erik.

"No!" Ms. Slaviero was starting to sound irritated. "More like: truth versus fiction, and how to tell whether a story comes from a reliable source or not."

Charlie groaned. "How do teachers do that?"

"Do what?" said Amelia as they joined the crowd heading to the classroom.

"Take something as awesome as a fight about aliens and turn it into the world's most boring lesson."

But as far as Amelia was concerned, the quicker they got off the topic of aliens, the better. She was good at keeping secrets, but she was a terrible liar – if anyone asked her if she believed in aliens, it wouldn't matter what she said. The truth would show clearly in her face.

And what would happen if, even as a joke, someone asked her if she'd ever *seen* an alien? Worse still, what if they asked *Charlie?*

For a while, it seemed like the whole thing might just blow over.

Despite Charlie's whining, Ms. Slaviero was one of those teachers who could make anything fun. Twenty minutes later, she had the interactive whiteboard covered with ideas and arrows, with words circled in purple or slashed through in red, or surrounded by green question marks.

By this time, the class had settled down. Amelia had felt the atmosphere in the room calm and cool as Ms. Slaviero taught them the difference between facts, theories and inferences. Even Callan and Erik were concentrating, their argument forgotten.

And then Ms. Slaviero wrecked it all.

"So let's look at this aliens-in-Egypt story together," she said, bringing her web browser up on the board.

Amelia's leg jiggled under the table. Charlie leaned over his desk in anticipation.

Ms. Slaviero typed into her search engine, and

then gave a little *Oh* of surprise at the results. Skimming down the page, Amelia saw how good the sources were – *Science Today,* the Egyptian *National News* website, the major news services in England, the USA, China, Germany, Canada, just for starters.

It's not a hoax ...

Amelia hadn't seen or heard any news that morning, of course. The headland where the hotel was built was so strongly magnetic, they couldn't use a TV, radio, computer, or even a mobile phone anywhere.

A sick feeling was growing in her stomach. It wasn't a fact, but she was starting to develop a theory of her own ... The more she thought about it, the more likely it seemed that all those phone calls her dad had been getting that morning were somehow connected to whatever had happened in Egypt.

Ms. Slaviero clicked on a link and the board became a big TV screen showing a video of a news crew at what looked like an archaeological dig. A pyramid was glowing pink in the background as the setting sun hit it, and a very excited reporter was speaking directly to the camera.

"An astonishing discovery – absolutely, this will rock our understanding of the history of Ancient Egypt – perhaps our understanding of humanity itself ..."

The video cut to the bottom of the excavations. Little pegs and string markers showed exactly where they were in the vast hole that had been carved into the sand. Towering over the archaeologist who stood beside it was, quite clearly, a crash-landed spaceship.

CHAPTER TWO

Charlie yelped in delight.

Amelia stared. The spaceship was enclosed in a thick shell of rough glass, as though it had been so white-hot when it hit Earth that it melted the sand around it. It was buried in the ground at an angle, and Amelia wondered at the total lack of control that must have led to such a violent collision.

Where the glass had been chipped away by the archaeologists, she could see the gray-green hull of the spaceship itself. Enough had been uncovered to show the scorch marks where it had burned its way through our atmosphere, the dents and gouges where space debris had hit it, and then – most unmistakably – writing that was nothing like any human system Amelia had ever seen before.

She glanced sideways at Sophie T. to see if she still thought it was a hoax. Her mouth sagged open and her face was quite white. Sophie F. was frowning at the screen. Shani was sitting perfectly still, half smiling.

"Well," muttered Ms. Slaviero. "I'm obviously going to have to rethink my policy of listening only to disco hits in the car on the way to school."

When the home bell finally rang, Amelia ran out the door so fast she accidentally knocked over the trash can. Charlie was right behind her, and up ahead she could see that her not-quite-a-dog, Grawk, was waiting in the shade of an oleander bush, his yellow eyes glowing.

"You know," she puffed as they ran along the beach road, "for a minute there, when Callan started yelling, I almost thought –"

"That it was me shooting my mouth off," Charlie said bluntly. But he wasn't offended.

Amelia shrugged. "Sorry."

"No chance," he went on. "Nothing I've ever said or done has ever impressed anyone around here."

That sounded horrible to Amelia.

Charlie wasn't feeling sorry for himself. "So you know how I'm getting my revenge on them all?"

"No."

He grinned. "Now that I have the coolest, most unbelievable, most impressive news ever, in the whole universe, literally, I'll *never tell them anything.*"

She laughed with him, but felt a little pang, too.

Then she didn't have enough breath for anything but running as the path started its steep climb up to the headland. By the time they reached the top of the hotel's long driveway, Amelia was too weary to pay much attention to the number of cars parked there. And when she and Charlie had chucked their bags down on the veranda and crashed through the hotel's main doors, she didn't stop to think before yelling out in the lobby, "Mum! Dad! There are aliens in Egypt!"

As her eyes adjusted to the dim indoor light, she realized that there was a line of complete strangers standing at the reception desk.

Ah, she thought as they all turned to stare. *Those would be guests.*

A man in a black suit and bowler hat paused with his room key in his hand, his forehead wrinkled in perplexity. The woman behind him scowled at Amelia, and pulled her two little children close, as though Amelia's bad manners might be catching. And the old lady behind her just looked too tired to be kept waiting any longer.

Behind the desk, Mum raised her eyebrows and said nothing.

Oops. The hotel had officially opened for business this week, which meant that for the first time, regular human tourists were coming to stay at the hotel, as well as the aliens that had been coming all along, disguised with holo-emitters. Amelia had only recently gotten used to the idea that the hotel really was her home, and now it had all changed again, and she had to get used to strangers living in the hotel with them.

"Dad is at Tom's," said Mum pointedly. "Why don't you –?"

Amelia and Charlie were back out the door and running down the hill before Mum could even finish the sentence.

Tom, the caretaker, lived at the bottom of the hotel grounds, behind a wall of ancient magnolia trees. He had a little wooden cottage in a clearing that just happened to be directly on top of the natural cave system where the gateway opened.

"Hey!" yelled Tom, as they burst through his door.

The tiny cottage seemed full of people. For the second time in two minutes, a group of adults turned to her. Amelia could have kicked herself. At least this time Dad was there too, grinning cheerfully. Beside him, an extremely old, wrinkly woman bent over her cane with her gray hair pinned up in a bun.

"Hello, here's trouble," she cackled.

"Ms. Rosby!" said Amelia.

"What are you doing here?" asked Charlie.

A square-shaped man with very short hair snorted disapprovingly.

"I can't believe you don't already know, Charlie," said Ms. Rosby. "I thought you two knew everything around here before anyone else."

The square man narrowed his eyes.

"What –?" Charlie began.

"Why, the starship in Egypt, of course!" said Ms. Rosby.

"That's quite enough, Rosby!" snapped the square man.

"That's what we came to tell you," said Charlie. "We saw it on the news at school."

"You see, Arxish?" Ms. Rosby smiled sweetly. "Hardly a secret, is it?"

Amelia had heard of Arxish before. He, Ms. Rosby and someone called Stern were the Big Three – Gateway Control's top alien agents stationed on Earth. Ms. Rosby had helped Amelia's family out of a tough spot before, when a guest had made a serious complaint against them.

She not only made sure that Dad and Tom kept their jobs, she'd also given official permission for Amelia and Charlie to be included in the gateway's secrets. She was rather fond of the two kids, actually. Despite her old-lady appearance, she was only six years old herself.

Arxish, though, was quite a different person.

Dad had said very little about him in front of Amelia, but she had gathered enough clues here and there to know he was one of the Control agents who believed the gateway should be taken away from humans and put directly under the authority of Control.

From the looks on their faces, the other two agents in the room agreed with Arxish. Amelia didn't know how Dad could be so happy knowing he was surrounded by aliens who thought he was nothing more than an ignorant, half-wit Earthling.

"Tell Mum I won't be home for dinner," he beamed.

"Ready, Walker?" said Arxish, holding out a strange clockwork steering wheel. Ms. Rosby and the other two crowded around and held on, leaving space for Dad's hand.

"Ready for what?" said Charlie.

Already Dad had taken hold of the wheel. It hummed, its center spun, and a swirl of light blossomed out, enveloping all five beings touching it. They flared green for a second and then vanished, leaving Amelia, Charlie and Tom staring at empty air.

CHAPTER THREE

Amelia and Charlie were still standing dumbfounded when the door to the cottage opened again. James thudded in, bright red in the face and puffing.

"I'm putting a lock on that door!" snapped Tom.

"Did I miss him?" James gasped.

"Do any of you kids know how to knock?" Tom pushed past Charlie and went to his desk, rifling through his papers. "This is my home, you know. Do any of you think of that?"

"Sorry, Tom," said James. "You're right."

"Don't see me bursting into *your* rooms," Tom muttered to himself.

James pushed his hair off his face and fanned himself, panting. "Dad's gone, I take it?"

"Yep," said Amelia.

"How?"

"Good question," said Charlie. "What *was* that thing?"

"Teleporter," Tom sniffed. "The show-offs. They'll want to be careful, zapping into Giza at sunrise with half the world's film crews on standby."

"A teleporter!" James's face broke into a goofy grin. "I wish I'd seen it. How does it work? It can't be electrical, can it, with all this magnetic interference –"

Tom sighed. "Was there something you wanted, James?"

James shrugged and looked around Tom's cottage. "Just ... you know ... wondered if there was anything I could ... help with?"

Amelia smiled to herself. It had taken several weeks and a face full of toxic Lellum slug mucus to make James believe that the aliens in this place were even *real*. But since then, all his science-geek/mad-inventor/gadget-genius circuits had kicked in, and he'd been driving Tom crazy, trying to learn everything he could about the gateway.

Tom gazed at him, one stony eye fixed on James and the other hidden beneath a black eye patch. "If you really want to help, you can put my charts in order."

It was quite obvious to Amelia that this was the sort of offer that was supposed to send James running back up the hill, but instead James looked as excited as a kid on his birthday.

"Thanks, Tom! You're the best!"

Tom grunted, and turned back to Amelia and Charlie. "Now, what do you want?"

"We just wanted to see what was happening," said Charlie.

"Well, don't look at me. You think anyone tells me anything? Rosby might have, if she'd come here on her own, but Arxish won't say a word. As far as he let slip to your dad, Control want to cover up this whole situation."

"Why?" said Amelia.

"We're a non-stellar planet, aren't we?" said Tom. "Never left our own solar system. So far as they're concerned, we might as well be living in caves and trying to make fire."

"But *we* know," said Charlie.

"Exactly," said Tom, and before either Amelia or Charlie could ask him what he meant by that, a gust of wind blew out of the gateway stairwell, flooding the cottage with the smell of grilled cheese. A wormhole had just connected to the gateway, opening up a path to an alien world.

Grawk, who had been lurking outside the cottage all this time, now wandered in, sniffing the air appreciatively.

"*More* guests?" said Charlie, straining to see what was happening in the other room.

"What do you expect?" said James casually. "We're a hotel."

"But there's already a line at the front desk!" said Charlie. "Also, since when are *you* so –?"

"Shh!" said Amelia. Whoever was coming through, she didn't want the first sound they heard on Earth to be Charlie complaining about them. Still, she understood what he meant. So far, they'd only ever had one or two groups of guests coming through the hotel at a time, and already that had been more than enough to deal with. What would it be like when the place really started to fill up?

"Hey," said James, unrolling a chart and squinting at it. "Am I reading this wrongly, or is this connection an hour and a half early?"

Rather than answering, Tom just grumbled and went to his drawer of holo-emitters, pulling one out for the new arrival. Once the holo-emitter was activated, it was impossible to tell who was really human and who was just faking it.

Amelia heard footsteps coming from the stairwell and, despite everything, felt a shiver of excitement. She didn't think she'd ever get bored of seeing what amazing creature came through the gateway next.

The visitor's head emerged from the stairwell in Tom's other room – a neat, pretty scarf tied over its hair, and a nice, oval face beneath.

Amelia frowned slightly. As the alien appeared, step-by-step, Amelia's disappointment grew. A plain navy-blue jacket. Nicely polished nails

at the end of ten fingers. Two hands and two ordinary arms. A pair of legs in navy trousers ended not in flippers, tentacles or robotic wheels, but two neat leather shoes. She was so ... *ordinary*.

"You're *human*," Charlie gasped.

The woman turned and glared at Charlie. She was plainly offended, but Amelia didn't know why.

But she can't be human, Amelia thought. Humans came from Earth – and there was only one Earth. Wasn't there?

Tom limped towards the guest. "Hello, I see you've brought your own holo-emitter. Do you mind if I check to see if it's correctly set to our sun's wavelength? Or if you'd rather I didn't alter yours, perhaps you would like to use one of mine?"

After Amelia got over the amusement of hearing Tom doing his polite voice, she realized how silly she'd been. Now she thought about it, of course a regular traveler would want their own holo-emitter. They must come in handy on all sorts of planets, not just Earth, and if you had your own, you could actually design your avatar for yourself instead of just picking from whatever Tom had stored on his.

The woman's scowl only deepened as Tom spoke. In fact, she looked more offended by Tom's offer of help than she had by Charlie's outburst. Lifting her chin, she swept past them all, striding through the cottage in her sensible shoes and out the door to the hotel grounds, as though it were beneath her dignity even to acknowledge anyone had spoken to her.

Amelia caught one last whiff of parmesan, and then the visitor was gone. For once, neither she nor Charlie made a move to follow or escort her to the hotel. Not only had the woman been rude, but Amelia wondered for a second if she might actually be bad. Not Krskn-level evil, perhaps, but a problem.

Grawk didn't seem fazed, though. He sat in the doorway and gazed dreamily after the woman, his tongue lolling out the side of his mouth as he breathed in her cheesy aroma. Amelia felt slightly better. Grawk had never been wrong so far.

CHAPTER FOUR

With Dad in Egypt, it was up to James and Mary to run the kitchen that night. Usually that wouldn't have been too much effort – but tonight, between the five human guests that had arrived that afternoon (including the two children, who turned out to be extremely picky eaters), and that one snooty alien woman, and Lady Naomi, their permanent resident, the hotel was the busiest it had ever been.

Lady Naomi rarely ate in the dining room with everyone else. Usually she was off somewhere doing her mysterious "research" – but since their run-in with Krskn last week, she'd become a bit more sociable. Teaming up to avoid getting kidnapped by an evil alien mercenary had a way of bringing people together. Amelia wouldn't exactly say they were *friends* yet – she was still a little starstruck by Lady Naomi – but she thought Lady Naomi liked them, too.

So it seemed quite natural when Lady Naomi sat at their table in the dining room. Even so, Amelia sat up straighter and remembered to tuck her elbows in.

"Hello, hello," said Lady Naomi in a low voice. "Am I interrupting something?"

"Of course not," said Amelia, afraid she'd move somewhere else.

"We're trying to figure out why that guy in the bowler hat keeps staring at us," Charlie said. "And whether humans evolved on Earth or actually arrived here through the gateway from some other part of the universe, and where that spaceship in Egypt came from, and what Amelia's dad is up to over there."

"Shh!" said Amelia, glancing over at the man in the bowler hat, who was still watching them intently. He sat a couple of feet away at the next table, but somehow she felt sure he was listening to every word they said. In fact, he was concentrating so hard on them, he hadn't noticed he'd dripped gravy down his suit jacket.

Perhaps he was from Control – one of Arxish's people, trying to prove that humans couldn't run the gateway correctly and should never have any contact with aliens.

Charlie opened his mouth to respond but before he could say a word, Lady Naomi said something so unexpected, it stopped him in his tracks.

"I don't suppose you'd like to come out to my research station and see if we can find out?"

Charlie would have bolted out the door there and then, but Lady Naomi insisted on having her dinner first.

"But it's already getting dark," he whined.

Lady Naomi just smiled.

"Oh, right." He slumped in his chair. "I forgot – you can see in the dark, can't you?"

Amelia kicked him under the table and flicked another quick look over at Bowler Hat Man. Luckily he seemed to be too busy sawing through a rock-hard roast potato to have heard Charlie. She was about to breathe a sigh of relief when she noticed that the woman in the scarf was now staring at them instead.

Why now? Amelia wondered. She didn't want

anything to do with them before.

Lady Naomi gave Charlie a stern look, and said to Amelia, "I'll go up and order my dinner at the window. It looks like James and Mary are far too busy to wait on tables tonight."

She rose from her chair and weaved between the tables of guests, as graceful as ever, even in the hiking boots and cargo pants she always wore.

Lady Naomi was a quiet person – short, slim and sort of neatly made. There was nothing about her that was flashy or asked for attention, and yet Amelia thought she was the most watchable person in the world. Partly it was her beautiful face, partly it was the terrible silvery scar that twisted down the length of her right arm, but mostly it was a sense of perfect stillness about her – as though she were always balancing on an invisible tightrope. Or as though she had her own gravity field inside her, so that wherever she went, she was the center of everything.

Sometimes, when Amelia tried to analyze just what it was about Lady Naomi that was so fascinating, she thought perhaps she was being silly and making it up. But right now, as the woman with the scarf watched Lady Naomi pass Amelia, she wasn't so sure. All of her arrogance was gone. She stared after Lady Naomi with almost ... desperation?

The guy in the bowler hat was watching them again, too. Waiting for Charlie to say something else he shouldn't.

"I think we should wait for you in the lobby," Amelia said as Lady Naomi got back to the table.

"Actually," said Lady Naomi, "it would probably be a good idea for you both to put on some long pants and decent shoes, while you're waiting for me."

"But aren't we just going down to the lab in the

caves?" said Charlie.

Lady Naomi shook her head. "You'll see."

Charlie followed Amelia into her bedroom and flopped down on her bed – her new/old one. That is, her parents had finally replaced the mattress on the big four-poster bed that had been in the room when they'd arrived. They'd even gotten her new curtains for it.

"I'm so sick of waiting for adults," Charlie moaned. "No matter how exciting something is, they can never just go *now*. It's always like, 'Yeah, Charlie, I already *said* we're going now – in twenty minutes.'"

Grawk, who'd been sleeping on a cushion in the bay window, yawned and wagged his tail when Amelia came over. She got her jeans and some thick socks and pushed Charlie off her bed.

"Move," she said, drawing the curtains on all four sides and enclosing herself. "I'm getting changed."

"What about me?" he said from outside the curtains.

"You can wear my sweatpants, if you want."

She smiled as he grumbled to himself, and when she finished changing, she called out, "Ready?" before opening the curtains.

Amelia smiled again to see him standing, quite dignified, in her black sweatpants. A nice pink stripe ran down one leg, and a fat pink daisy was embroidered on one hip. He had his back to her, and was staring at the little safe door on Amelia's other wall. As if looking serious and thoughtful about how to unlock it would distract Amelia from the cute little row of diamanté that sparkled across his bottom.

He turned and glared at her. "Say nothing."

They hurried downstairs to the lobby, Grawk padding ahead of them. Mum was on the phone behind the reception desk.

She covered the receiver with one hand. "Where do you think you're going?"

"Oh, I hope you don't mind, Skye," said Lady Naomi, coming from the dining room. "I asked them if they'd like to go for a walk with me. I won't keep them long."

Mum instantly relaxed. "Oh, no problem, then. Be good, you two." Her attention was pulled back to her phone conversation. "Yes, I'm here, Mr. Snavely. The question is –"

Amelia and Charlie followed Lady Naomi out of the hotel, down the main steps and across the sloping lawns, almost in the direction of the hedge maze.

"Are we going into the bush?" asked Charlie.

Neither he nor Amelia had explored the bush

side of the headland yet. There was so much to discover in the hotel itself, not to mention the steady stream of alien guests, that they hadn't bothered to investigate past the maze. And the bush was so dense with spiky, scratchy trees, thorny bushes and cutting grasses, and so full of biting, stinging creatures everywhere, that it hardly invited you in for a nice bush walk.

Lady Naomi led the kids to a shaggy old banksia tree, checked behind them, and then pulled aside a low-hanging branch.

In the grass behind it was a path. If Amelia had found it by herself, she would have thought it had been made by wombats and ignored it, but now Lady Naomi was urging them on. Grawk ran ahead, his nose to the ground, his tail up like an antenna.

"You do your research *here?*" said Charlie.

"Yes. Well, not here exactly. I have to go quite

a bit farther to get away from the headland's magnetism before I can use my equipment."

"Oh," said Amelia. "That's why. We always thought you went away because what you're doing is so top secret."

"That too!" Lady Naomi laughed, then paused as if listening for something. They stood silently for several long seconds, then Lady Naomi shook her head and kept walking. "So how much did your dad tell you about that starship in Egypt?"

"Nothing," said Amelia.

"Really?" Lady Naomi pressed her. "Nothing at all?"

"He didn't have time to tell us anything," said Charlie. "He just whooshed away with those Control freaks." He snorted. "Hey, get it? *Control freaks?*"

"Ms. Rosby's not a freak," said Amelia.

"Yes, she is," said Charlie. "I mean, she's cool

and stuff, but come on – she's six years old and looks like Santa's grandma. That is actually, literally freaky. Admit it."

"So you don't know any more about the starship than what was on the news?" Lady Naomi said.

Amelia suddenly wondered just why Lady Naomi had brought them out here. She'd been so careful up until now to keep all her comings and goings private, and she'd done such a good job that Amelia hadn't even had a clue which direction she went in. And now she was inviting them in? That seemed like more than just friendliness. And now, from Lady Naomi's questions, it seemed as though she'd been hoping to find out something from them that would ...

Well, she didn't know what Lady Naomi wanted. Information about the spaceship? Or about Control's interest in it? Did she think there was some connection between the crashed ship and whatever it was that she was researching out here?

They turned a corner, the light now so dim that the colors had almost completely faded out of the landscape. Amelia stumbled over a root, then straightened up to see they'd reached a small clearing in the trees. In the middle of the clearing was a huge granite boulder.

"Here we are," said Lady Naomi.

"What do you want us to do?" said Charlie. "Climb up and look for Egypt from there?"

"Not quite." Lady Naomi took a little device from her pocket and the boulder vanished. In its place was a small workstation – a desk made up of various screens and keyboards, like something halfway between a jumbo jet's cockpit and the computers from Dad's old job with the government. None of it was human technology, though. Maybe it was the strange sounds and weird glow that gave it away.

Not that it mattered. It had come as a surprise when Krskn didn't know what species Lady Naomi was, but Amelia hadn't ever thought being an alien was a reason not to trust or like someone. And yet, she couldn't help feeling a prickle of unease as she looked at Lady Naomi's equipment and realized that every piece had been brought to Earth to study ... *what?* What *was* Lady Naomi getting up to out here?

"This is amazing!" Charlie said. "But what do you do when it rains?"

Lady Naomi pressed a button and a holo-roof flashed into position overhead. "Want to see what all this can do?"

Amelia and Grawk drew closer and watched as Lady Naomi brought her machinery to life. She entered a series of passwords and scanned her fingerprints and retinas before an enormous holo-screen lit up. Amelia gasped. The bush was hidden from them by a vast image of Earth – the whole globe rotating in space.

Lady Naomi put her hands into a pair of holographic gloves and began to manipulate the image, turning the planet until she found Africa, then zooming in to Egypt. Amelia saw the Nile winding like a piece of green string against a pale yellow background. As Lady Naomi zoomed in tighter again, Amelia realized this wasn't a computer generated *map* – this was a real satellite image. She could even see cars and trucks moving along the road. The image drew closer until she could see the texture of the roads themselves, and the dry grasses growing beside them.

"Are you a hacker?" Amelia asked. "Is this all government spy satellites?"

"Don't worry," said Lady Naomi. "It's all perfectly legal."

Amelia noticed that she hadn't answered her

question. Lady Naomi didn't even say which laws she was obeying – Earth's? Control's? Or someone else's?

"All right," Lady Naomi murmured to herself. "We know it's near one of the pyramids of Giza ..."

"Underneath one," Charlie corrected.

Lady Naomi clicked her tongue, a disappointed kind of sound. "Truly ancient, then. If it crashed into the ground *before* the pyramids were built, then it must have been there for over five thousand years." She sighed. "Oh, well, let's see for ourselves ..."

It wasn't hard to work out which pyramid they wanted. A black perimeter fence with orange flags had been set up around the corner of one, and the fence itself was now surrounded by cars, vans, film crews, tourists and their tour buses, and local people who were either keen to get a glimpse or to sell drinks and snacks to those who were.

Lady Naomi zoomed in to the center of the fenced area. The whole dig had been roofed in with a black tarpaulin. Charlie groaned.

"No, no, this was to be expected," Lady Naomi said. "They know that every single kid with a camera and a drone helicopter will try to get a shot."

"What then?" said Charlie.

Grawk grumbled beside Amelia and shifted around to gaze into the bush. It was completely dark by now, and Amelia couldn't see what had caught his attention. Probably a possum up a tree.

"Look at this," said Lady Naomi. The image changed from the natural colors of the desert to a dull blue gray. The dig site, though, was different. An oblong shape glowed red.

"What's that?" said Amelia.

"Radioactivity," said Lady Naomi.

"It's a nuclear bomb?" Charlie gaped.

"Not that kind of radioactivity," Lady Naomi

went on. "Everything has some radioactivity, even you and I do. I've asked the computer to screen out every expected radioactive signature, which is why the screen is basically all blue. But this red – well, that's a radioactive signature that is out of time, and out of place."

"Alien?" said Charlie.

"Definitely."

Another click, and the holo-screen became completely black, before quickly filling with tiny green dots. The dots were grouped together in one place, with some slowly drifting away from the group, and others coming in to join it.

"What are the dots?" said Charlie. "People?"

"Close," said Lady Naomi. "They're phones."

"You can see a dot for every mobile phone?"

"Yes, and ..." Lady Naomi typed at the keyboard, and some of the green dots disappeared. "That removed the phones without cameras. And this ..."

Half the dots turned red. "This shows which phones have taken video in the last fifteen minutes." She beamed at the kids. "Who wants to see what those guys are filming down there?"

Amelia did. But she was also slightly freaked out by what Lady Naomi was doing. Could she really get into the memory of any mobile phone on the planet? Did that mean she could also look into any computer? And why would she want to do that? She thought about Callan shouting about the Illuminati, and wondered if it was really all that crazy an idea ...

Grawk let out a sharp bark of warning as a branch snapped under someone's foot, just outside the workstation.

Lady Naomi pressed a button and the holo-screen vanished. The whole clearing lit up as halogen lights flared. All three of them swung around to see who the intruder was.

Grawk scampered away from the workstation and over to the figure, frozen in the light, her usually neat scarf pulled awry on her head.

CHAPTER FIVE

"You!" said Charlie. "You followed us!"

The woman in the scarf ran towards them.

"What do you want?" Lady Naomi demanded.

Amelia braced herself, waiting for some proud, angry retort. To her surprise, though, the woman couldn't have been meeker or more apologetic.

"I'm so sorry," she said. "I overheard you with the children at the hotel ..."

Lady Naomi was stone-faced, her hands on her hips. "Yes?"

The woman nervously straightened her scarf.

"You mentioned that you could find out about the starship in Egypt ..."

Amelia noticed Grawk sniffing delicately at the woman's shoe.

"Well, you see," the woman said miserably, realizing that no one was about to make things easy for her, "I've lost my husband, and I wondered if you could help me find him?"

"What's your husband got to do with us?" said Charlie. "Is he an Egyptian archaeologist?"

Lady Naomi crossed her arms, clearly wary. "Yes, go on. Why do you think I can help you?"

"I thought ..." The woman wrung her hands. "I don't know. I came here to find him myself, but then when I heard you offer to help find the children's father ... I wondered ..."

Lady Naomi frowned, unmoved. Then Amelia realized that Lady Naomi didn't know one crucial fact about the woman in the scarf.

"She came through the gateway," Amelia blurted. "She already looked human when she came up the stairs, but Charlie and I saw her arrive."

"Oh." Lady Naomi relaxed slightly. At least she wouldn't be breaking Control's rules by having the woman there.

But knowing the woman had come through the gateway wasn't the same as knowing who she was, so Amelia understood when Lady Naomi ignored the tears in the other woman's eyes and asked, "Who is your husband? How did he get lost?"

The woman swallowed hard and ducked her head, but she didn't look surprised by Lady Naomi's series of questions. Disappointed maybe, but a disappointment she had expected. When she raised her face again, it was still streaked with tears, but now there was a kind of bitter resignation to it.

She almost smiled as she said, "I don't suppose you'll believe me if I say I can't tell you."

"Not really," said Charlie. "I mean, for all we know, you could be Mrs. Krskn. He's the only alien we've seen getting lost lately."

Like every other alien Amelia had ever met, the woman in the scarf balked at the mention of Krskn.

"No, not him, I promise you. But if there was any way I could use your equipment on my own ... for only the shortest time ..."

"No." Lady Naomi was firm. "Not a chance."

"Not even if –" the woman began.

"No. But if you're willing to give me the information ..."

The woman held up a hand. "No, I understand. Neither of us can bend to the other on this. Never mind. I will find another way. Please excuse my interruption."

Without another word, she turned and walked into the bush, disappearing into the darkness.

Walking to school the next day with Charlie, Amelia was still trying to figure it out. Grawk padded beside her like a shadow.

"She was definitely telling the truth," she said. "You could tell she wasn't faking being upset about her husband. But she's making it impossible for anyone to help her. Which makes me think that at least one of them is in trouble. Like, on the run from the law or something ..."

Charlie kicked a stone on the path and grunted. He really couldn't care less about some alien's relationship problems – and, as he'd been saying all morning, he couldn't understand why *she* cared either, when all of humanity might be about to find proof of the existence of aliens.

"Or maybe," Amelia went on, "she can't say anything because her husband's here as a spy, and she doesn't want to blow his cover. Oh!" She turned to Charlie with a new thought. "Maybe it *does* connect with Egypt – maybe her husband is one of the Control agents that went with Dad to check out the spaceship."

Charlie snorted. "Well, he's hardly lost, then, is he? She knows exactly where he is."

"Unless there's some other reason they can't be together ..."

"Urgh! Maybe he's not lost because he's running

away from her, did you think of that? Maybe she's in love with him, and he thinks she's a big, crazy, crying *stalker* lady. Maybe we should be helping him *stay* escaped from her."

Amelia shook her head at Charlie.

The bell rang and Grawk turned without a sound and headed back to the hotel.

"Hurry up, you two!" Ms. Slaviero called. "There's a special news bulletin about Egypt in ten minutes."

Amelia and Charlie pelted into class along with the rest of the kids. Even Sophie T., despite her sarcasm the day before, was excited to see what else the archaeologists had found out.

"Righty-ho, guys," Ms. Slaviero grinned, as she powered up the board. "Let's see what's new on planet Earth. I mean, *ancient* – thousands of years old, obviously – but new for us."

Amelia fidgeted in her seat. There had been

no phone calls from Dad last night or this morning. Mum said that was fine and totally to be expected. Not only was Dad probably too busy with Control to even eat, let alone make phone calls, there was a nine-hour time difference between Egypt and Australia. Which was fine. But she wished she knew what this announcement was going to be.

She heard the sound of soft chanting and saw Charlie and Erik grinning as they crossed all the fingers on both hands and rocked in time to the words, "Be aliens! Be aliens! Be aliens!"

To one side of them, Callan was white-faced with fear.

Ms. Slaviero went to a news channel, and the screen was filled with jostling reporters. They weren't at the dig site, but in a bland conference room. Several people walked onto the stage and hundreds of cameras clicked and flashed as the chief archaeologist stood by a microphone. She looked exhausted (it was after midnight in Egypt), but also very, very excited.

Amelia curled her toes inside her shoes and held her breath. Sophie T. gripped her arm.

The chief archaeologist spoke in English. "The artifact found under the northeastern corner of the Great Pyramid has now been completely excavated and removed from the site."

She clicked a button, and the projector screen behind her lit up with an image of the pyramid and the dig site. "As you can see, in order to access the artifact, we had to dig under the pyramid itself. The structural difficulties of doing this without compromising the pyramid above have slowed our work considerably. Although news of the artifact has only just broken for you all here," she smiled at the reporters, "my team has in fact been digging this site for nearly a year."

Get on with it, Amelia thought.

"As you can see here …" The picture on the screen changed. "The artifact was found encased in a crude glass shell, some six to eight inches thick. It appears the artifact may have been buried while hot enough to melt the surrounding sand –"

"Spaceship – spaceship – spaceship –" Charlie and Erik whispered in unison.

"As yet we have no theories as to how or why this heating may have occurred. The glass has now been pried off, allowing my team to fully inspect the artifact itself."

The cameras clicked and flashed in excitement.

"It is an object unlike any other previously dug up in Egypt or indeed, any other place on Earth."

The cameras were going crazy now.

"This discovery demands that we rewrite everything we have believed about our history, our origins, about our very identity as human beings …"

The cameras couldn't shoot any faster. Amelia had clenched every muscle in her body so tightly it was painful. Sophie T.'s grip on her arm was like iron.

"The artifact," the chief archaeologist said proudly, "dates back at least six thousand years, and is undoubtedly the most beautiful, sophisticated, and advanced sarcophagus we have ever seen."

"*What!?*" Charlie shouted.

A similar reaction spread through the crowd of reporters on the screen. Hands shot into the air.

The chief archaeologist smiled wryly. You could tell she knew exactly what was coming. She pointed at one reporter. "Yes?"

"So it's not an alien spacecraft?" he called out.

"No."

"How can you be sure?" another reporter yelled.

"By being scientific and using the facts available to us," she said calmly. "And not getting swept up in fairy tales!"

The reporters began to shout more questions, but she plowed on. "The artifact is made of a green chrysoprase stone, not particularly common, but a perfectly normal Earth mineral. Its surface shows marks of iron cutting tools – *human* cutting tools," she added fiercely. "We have more testing to do, but we are convinced –"

Amelia blocked out her voice, thinking hard. The archaeologist was either wrong, or lying! Lady Naomi had shown them a radioactive reading that was impossible for an Earth-made object. And what about those pockmarks and burns where it had been damaged in Earth's atmosphere? Not to mention the little fact it plummeted into the ground so fast it burned its way through the sand ... And what sophisticated, powerful pharaoh was ever buried at an angle like that? Hardly a decent burial!

No, she wouldn't believe it. And she *was* using

the facts available to her.

Nobody else in the class had been won over, either.

"That's all lies!" shouted Erik. "They tried to tell us crop circles were made by humans, too!"

Amelia saw Charlie struggling to contain himself.

She thought Callan at least would be pleased, but he was just as angry as Erik. "It's a cover-up! They want us to stay blind to the invasion until it's all over!"

Ms. Slaviero switched off the board. "All right. All right, settle down."

"I knew it wasn't aliens." Sophie T. blew her bangs off her face and grinned. "I know the boys wanted it to be like *Star Wars* was real, but really, just another stone coffin makes a lot more sense."

But that's just it, Amelia thought, smiling weakly. *It doesn't make any sense at all.*

When Amelia and Charlie got back to the hotel that afternoon, their mums were talking together in low voices in the lobby.

"I don't know how much longer to wait," said Amelia's mum.

"Until dinnertime?" Mary suggested. "Then, if he still doesn't come out, we can knock and offer him room service."

"Hey," said Charlie. "What's up?"

Mum looked around to make sure they weren't being overheard. "We might have a problem with one of the guests."

"That woman with the bratty kids?" said Charlie. "She's horrible. We just saw her on the driveway, and she practically wet herself when Grawk walked past her little girl."

"Shh!" said Mary. "Don't be so rude! Or at least,

not so loud."

"No, not her," said Mum. "The nice older man in the bowler hat. He hasn't left his room since dinner last night. We're worried he's been taken ill and needs a doctor, but he hasn't phoned for help and he's got the Do Not Disturb sign on his door, so we're not sure how long to leave him until we knock."

The main doors of the lobby opened and in came James (home early from school – it must have been one of his early afternoons) followed by –

"Dad!" Amelia cried. "You're back!"

So were the rest of the Control crew. Amelia expected them all to be as gruff and stern as they had been in Tom's cottage, but they were quite cheerful. Even Arxish looked almost friendly. Things must have gone really well in Egypt.

Wait – what?

Amelia was more puzzled than ever.

"Hey, cookie," Dad grinned. "Did you miss me? Do you want to see what we brought you back for a souvenir?"

"Is it a pyramid in a snow globe?" said Charlie.

"Nope." Dad's smile was so wide that Amelia could see all his teeth. "How about a freshly stolen alien starship?"

CHAPTER SIX

"Walker!" snapped Arxish, his moment of good humor gone in less than a second. "What did I say to you about Control protocols?"

"Ah, come on," said Dad easily. "It's only the kids. They already know about the gateway without any issues. You let them see us all teleport, for Pete's sake. What's the difference?"

"We even met Krskn," said Charlie, helpful as ever. He never seemed to get enough of watching aliens spasm at that name.

Arxish glowered, but Ms. Rosby slapped him

on the back. "Relax, Arxish. It's not as though any human alive will connect the thing in Egypt with what we're doing here with the gateway. Largely because there is no connection."

Arxish made a face as though he were about to argue with Ms. Rosby, but then Mum said, "Well, whatever you decide, can you talk about it somewhere else? I've got two regular guests upstairs, and more outside in the gardens."

Arxish flushed, embarrassed to be caught out like that.

"OK, great!" Dad clapped his hands together. "Well, come on, kids – want to see it now?"

Amelia and Charlie didn't bother to answer. Instead they ran across the lobby to the doors, James beside them, as they leapt down the steps to the lawn.

"Have you seen it already?" Amelia asked him.

"No, Dad wanted to wait for you."

Amelia looked back, and saw Dad patiently helping Ms. Rosby totter down the steps, her hand clutching tightly to Dad's arm while Arxish waited at the bottom holding her cane.

"Oh, we'll *never* get to it at this rate," muttered Charlie.

James smirked and shoved Charlie's shoulder. "Just wait till we're over the hill."

"Where are we going?" said Amelia, as Dad and Ms. Rosby reached them.

"Down to Lady Naomi's," said Dad. "She's been very generous and said we can use her shields until Control know what to do with it."

"But why did you steal it? The archaeologist thinks it's an Earth-made sarcophagus, so Control's secret is safe, isn't it?"

"That was the whole point of our mission!" said Dad, helping Ms. Rosby over the brow of the hill, and holding tightly to her arm.

Once the hotel was out of sight behind them, Ms. Rosby swung her cane over one shoulder, straightened her back and called out, "Keep up, lads!" as she sprinted down the hill, her bony knees flashing under the flapping hem of her dress.

Arxish ran after her, leaving the humans behind. Amelia and Charlie were desperate to catch up, but Dad held them back. Charlie didn't look too sure about staying behind.

From the other side of the hill, Grawk bounded up and pulled to a slow trot beside them.

"Don't worry," said Dad. "We won't miss anything, but if you want me to answer your questions, it's better to do it without Arxish overhearing us. Poor fellow is annoyed enough without us rubbing his face in it."

He yawned and scratched the red stubble on his chin, and then went on. "Control monitor all the archaeological and exploratory work on Earth. In fact, Arxish is the head of that whole department. So they've known for months what was coming, and had been steadily developing a plan to deal with it. What they didn't expect was the news to leak and speed up the dig before they'd made the swap."

"The swap?" said Charlie.

"Yes. Once the pod had been discovered, the archaeologists had to dig up *something*. Arxish has a very low opinion of humans in general, but even he admits that we would notice if a big, solid, buried-in-glass object simply vanished from under our shovels. On the other hand, Arxish is determined to keep all alien technology out of human hands."

"But why?" said Amelia. "We're not allowed to know about aliens until we discover them for ourselves, but we're not allowed to discover them either ... well, that's not fair."

"I know," said Dad. "I've had the same argument with Control more times than I can count. Ms. Rosby sees it our way, and thinks it can only be good for everyone – Control, Earth and all the travelers through the gateway – if humans know the full story. But Arxish and his faction have more votes, and they've convinced head office that we humans have to figure out interstellar space travel on our own first. Letting us get hold of an alien spaceship, they say, would unnaturally speed up our technology and science, and ... well, Arxish thinks he's protecting us from ourselves by keeping Earth ignorant."

"That's –" Amelia spluttered.

"That's cool, Mr. Walker," Charlie cut her off. "But what about the *spaceship?*"

"What about the swap?" James added.

"Right, right." They'd reached the end of the lawn, and Dad pulled aside the banksia branch to let the kids onto Lady Naomi's path. "They used the same teleporter that took us to Egypt to get the ship out of its glass casing. It was genius! They just beautifully folded the fourth dimension there and the ship slipped neatly into Lady Naomi's clearing here. So then the ship was safely away, but there was a huge glass cavity in the ground. Next they reversed the teleporter so that it worked like a kind of 3-D printer, and just filled in the space. And I mean, seamlessly! Down to every last wrinkle and bump in the glass. Just *beep-boop-bip*!" He mimed pressing buttons. "Type in *green chrysoprase*, upload your design, factor in the right radiation signature for the supposed age of the thing, and it's built almost instantly! From the electrons up! Job done, we go home, and the archaeologists of Egypt have a whole new career ahead of them! Everyone's a winner!"

"But we just got cheated out of our aliens,"

Charlie protested.

"Yes, well, there is that ... I can't say I like it, either, Charlie."

They trudged around the last bend and saw Arxish and Ms. Rosby standing beside an awkward-looking Lady Naomi. When she saw Dad and the kids, her face brightened and she came over to them at once. Amelia noticed Grawk had disappeared again.

"I'm not sure about this, Scott," Lady Naomi said in a low voice. "The starship is one thing, but I didn't agree to have this bunch take over my facility."

Dad patted her shoulder. "It'll only be a day or two at most. And Ms. Rosby and I will do our best to make sure Control come through with some upgraded equipment as a way of saying thanks."

Lady Naomi considered him, her frustration slowly giving way to a small smile. "All right. You've got me there. Just keep that Arxish away from me – he's obnoxious."

"So where's the spaceship?" said Charlie.

Amelia nudged him and pointed. Hadn't Charlie noticed? Lady Naomi's holo-rock was significantly larger than it had been.

"Where?" said Charlie.

Lady Naomi took out her little gadget and the rock vanished. This time, in front of the workstation, a large dark-green object hung in midair. It was somehow both bigger and smaller than Amelia had expected – about the size of a very large chest freezer. Quite enormous for a freezer, in fact, but not very big at all if you were inside it while blasting through space.

One part of her mind was simply astonished that a thing she had first seen in a faraway country on the news was now floating only feet from her. Another part of her was sort of deflated. It was nothing at all like the sleek, shiny, gorgeous-looking ships she'd seen in movies.

Charlie didn't appear to be disappointed. Or bothered by how the ship had glowed red on Lady Naomi's radiation scan. He walked right up to it and ran his hands over the burned surface. "Cool ..."

"Hey!" snapped one of the Control agents. "No touching!"

"Don't be ridiculous," Ms. Rosby said bluntly. "This thing has traveled light-years through space, survived asteroid belts, burned up through this planet's atmosphere, and survived a terminal velocity impact with the surface. What damage do you think the kid will inflict?"

The agent muttered to himself. "Yes, by all means," he said grimly. "Fondle the ship to your heart's content ... if we can't discover how to open it, how to read the writing on the sides, or how to determine its origin, why not let the human pup have a try?"

Amelia saw his mouth twist, and the other guy in the crew looked sullen, too. Clearly, this puzzle was too big even for Control.

Dad stayed out all night with the Control crew and Lady Naomi, trying to open the ship. At breakfast, he finally staggered in, but from the look on his face, Amelia knew they'd made little progress.

The man in the bowler hat came into the dining room behind Dad, and went straight to the table he'd sat at for dinner the first night. Amelia was pleased. She knew that Mum and Mary would be relieved he was OK. And he was OK, wasn't he? He was looking –

She jerked back in her chair and the butter knife in her hand banged so hard on the edge of the plate, she chipped it.

"What's up with you?" said Charlie, pausing between bites of toast.

Amelia whispered, "That's *not* Bowler Hat Man. It's the same hat, but it's not the same man."

Charlie peered at their neighbor. "Same suit, too. I recognize the gravy stains." He shrugged. "Maybe his holo-emitter is playing up. Or maybe he just decided he wanted to be better looking, and hoped no one would notice the change."

Charlie's explanation was so reasonable, Amelia was almost convinced. But he'd overlooked a vital fact.

"But the man in the bowler hat isn't an alien, Charlie. He didn't come through the gateway, and he didn't get a holo-emitter from Tom. Don't you remember? He came in a rental car like the other human guests. And his car is still outside the hotel!"

"But then …" Charlie's eyes widened. "If the guy didn't leave in his car, where is he?"

"And," said Amelia, "who is this guy? And what is he doing in the other guy's clothes?"

It was so disturbing, Amelia ran straight to tell her mother. Not that they could find her. Amelia tried the library, which Mum used as an office, her parents' bedroom, the kitchen, and even the ballroom. Eventually, they found Mary upstairs in the guest wing, making up beds.

"She went down to Tom's," said Mary. "She'll be back in a min–"

But Amelia and Charlie were already running. They knew better than to run madly through the lobby, so instead they went the other way, down the corridor to the back of the hotel where the servants' stairs led out to the grounds a secret way.

They got out to the ballroom deck and lawns just in time to see a black-hatted figure creeping

past the hedges. The fake Bowler Hat
Man, and he had one of the hotel's
giant laundry chute bags
over his shoulder. A *bag*.

One large, knobbly
object was crammed
into the bag, and
it looked exactly
the right size and
shape to be a
human body.

CHAPTER SEVEN

Amelia and Charlie froze, unable to believe what they had just seen. Or *thought* they had seen ...

As if they didn't have enough to think about between the alien spaceship and the weird scarf lady and Control sticking their nose in everything, now they had to deal with a –

Amelia stopped, not wanting to say the word *murderer*, even to herself.

Amelia tapped Charlie on the arm, then pointed to the other side of the hotel. If they were quick enough, they could run around the whole hotel and see where the impostor was going without the risk of following along behind. If that *was* a body in the bag, there was no way Amelia wanted to get caught spying.

Charlie nodded, and they sprinted as quietly as possible around to the front of the hotel, meeting Grawk on the way. Amelia put a finger to her lips to warn him they were being sneaky.

Looking out over the hotel grounds, they saw the top of the bowler hat just disappear below the brow of the hill as the man headed down to the bush. For a moment, Amelia was worried he was heading for Lady Naomi's workstation, but he was actually bearing farther left, more towards the maze.

Amelia, Charlie and Grawk were totally exposed, running across the open grass of the hill after him, with nowhere to hide and no way to pretend they were doing anything other than chasing him. But they had no choice. If they waited until he got to the bush before they started after him, they would lose the trail.

Luckily for them, he didn't turn to check behind him.

"I reckon that's the real Bowler Hat Man he's got in there," said Charlie quietly. "And now he's going to dump him in the bush."

"Listen!" Amelia whispered.

The man had started picking his way into the bush, and even from their distance, they could hear the crunching, snapping sound of leaves and twigs under each footstep.

"We can't follow him in there," she realized.

"We can't let him get away with murder!"

"No, but Charlie, he'll hear us from miles away if we go after him. And if he murdered the real Bowler Hat Man, what's to stop him murdering us too?"

Charlie paused over that, and then Amelia noticed Grawk wagging his tail and staring at her intently. Grawk, who had known Krskn was bad news before anyone else had any idea he was there. Grawk, who could tell it was Charlie even when he was disguised with a holo-emitter. Amelia still wasn't sure just what Grawk knew or how he knew it, but by now she was happy to trust his judgment.

And right now, Grawk looked as relaxed and pleased as Amelia had ever seen him. She nudged Charlie. "Look! He's on to something!"

Once Grawk had their attention, he took off – trotting through the grass with his head held high, sniffing the air, his ears cocked towards the bush.

"I think Grawk's tracking him," she said. "But not following him – look. He's working out where he's going."

Indeed, Grawk bounded twenty or more yards

downhill, sniffed and listened a bit more. Then he blinked solemnly at Amelia, and walked into the bush.

"Brilliant, Grawk," she whispered. "Look, Charlie. The bush is thinner here, and there are all those rocks ahead. If we're careful, we can get in there without making a sound."

"Get in where?" Charlie grumbled. "Grawk could be taking us to see his favorite peeing tree for all we know."

But Amelia could tell he didn't really mean it, and in fact, when they scrambled up the side of a boulder and saw the fake Bowler Hat Man walking along the bottom of the gully below them, Charlie didn't seem surprised.

The impostor was still carrying the laundry bag over his shoulder, and now Amelia noticed there was something odd in the way it hung across his back, bumping up and down with each step.

"It's not heavy enough to be a body," she whispered.

"Unless he's superstrong."

"Even then. The bag would still show strain under the weight. That bag looks like it's full of feathers."

The man looked around him, then wandered over to some thick bushes, whirled the bag around his head, and let it fly so that it arced up over the tips of the bushes, and landed hidden behind them. Without a backward glance, the man turned and walked back the way he'd come.

There was no sign that he'd suspected he had been watched, but still Amelia and Charlie waited ten long minutes before they went out to inspect the bag. A month or so ago, they might have just crashed their way through the undergrowth as soon as the man was out of sight. Now that they'd seen Krskn in action, they understood that these adventures that kept befalling them had no safety net. No time-outs, second chances, or places to regroup and try again. If this man were really a murderer, they couldn't afford to act like kids.

They waited until Grawk led the way out.

"You were right," said Charlie. "No matter how strong he was throwing that bag, it didn't sound heavy as it hit the trees."

They scrambled through the leaves and branches to get to the bag.

"But if it's not a body ..." Amelia began. "That means the real Bowler Hat Man is still missing."

"And whatever is in this bag," Charlie finished, "he still came all the way out here to dump it."

Grawk was at the bag already, wagging his tail and sniffing in delight.

Amelia took a sniff too. "Ugh!" Even from three feet away it was rank – sour milk and vomit.

Charlie poked the bag with a stick and the

end of it sank in without resistance. Amelia stretched out a foot and pressed on a bulge with her sneakered toe. It gave way like wadding or a folded blanket.

"So weird," said Charlie.

Amelia bent down and grabbed the edge of the bag. "Ready or not ..." she said, and yanked it open.

A gust of rancid, puke-flavored air engulfed them, strong enough to make them both cough. They held their noses and stared at the bag's contents.

"So ..." Charlie said at last. "What is that?"

The thing inside the laundry bag was so strange, it took Amelia several long moments to process what she was seeing. It was a pale yellowy color – that was the first thing that got through. Then she noticed how kind of *hairy* it was – like a huge, loose spool of wool, if the wool had been so fine it looked more like fiberglass. Strangest of all, Amelia saw that it was hollow and she was looking into it through a big gash along one side. It looked as though it had been violently torn open.

It definitely wasn't a body, but in its own way it was nearly as horrible. And although it was clearly alien, there was something weirdly familiar about it, as though Amelia had seen one of these before.

Except who would ever forget seeing one of these? Or smelling one? She shuddered.

"We have to tell Dad. Or Tom.

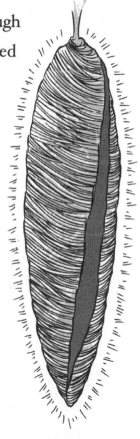

Probably Ms. Rosby, too."

"Can you imagine how angry Arxish will be?" Charlie said. He poked the bag again. "Do you think we should bring it with us?"

He bent down, reached into the bag and touched the woolly thing. "Oh, yuck! It's all sticky!" He wiped his hand on his pants.

"It doesn't look sticky," said Amelia. "Is it like cotton candy?"

"Almost," said Charlie. "Only much stickier, more like – oh! That's what it is! It's a spiderweb!"

They both looked in horror at the bag.

"That's what spiders do when they catch a bug," said Charlie in a low voice. "They wrap it up in silk and suck the guts out. I bet that's what happened to the real Bowler Hat Man. And that's why there's no body – the new guy already *ate* it."

But Amelia, sick with fear, shook her head and squatted down for a closer look at the empty wrappings. "I don't think that's it, Charlie ... I think it's much, much worse than that ..."

She pointed into the hollow space and Charlie crouched down beside her. "Look how clean it is inside. No one died in there or had their guts sucked out."

"Then what? You don't think Bowler Hat Man is dead?"

"Oh, no, I think he is – or *wishes* he was." Amelia closed her eyes. "I think this is an egg sac."

"An egg sac –" Charlie frowned. "But there are no eggs in there."

Amelia looked at him bleakly. "There wouldn't be – once they *hatched*."

Now Charlie turned a sickly green and gulped. "So the giant alien spider had babies, and they are ... in the hotel? And the real Bowler Hat Man ...?"

"Baby food," Amelia nodded. She flung a small

stick at Grawk, who was nibbling happily on the edge of the stinky silk sac. "Stop it! Bad dog!"

Grawk didn't turn around, but kicked back with one paw, showering Amelia with a little cloud of dirt, leaves and eucalyptus nuts.

"Fine," she snapped at him. "Be gross, then. Come on, Charlie."

"Come on *where?*" He followed her back up the gully to the rocks. "We're not going to the hotel, surely?"

"Tom's. He's got a phone. We can call the hotel and tell Mum and Mary to evacuate."

"This is a disaster."

Grawk got over his irritation with Amelia and soon caught up and started leading the way through the bush again. Amelia was grateful. She'd been so absorbed in being stealthy on the way down, she hadn't memorized the path. Plus, she couldn't deny it, she felt much safer having Grawk with them, just in case the alien spider daddy had actually sensed them spying on him and was now lying in wait behind a bush somewhere ...

But no one was waiting in ambush for them. No one tried to trap them. There was one bend in the track where Charlie walked face-first into an orb weaver's web and freaked out, clawing the strands off his cheeks and yelling, "Get off me, you sicko!" Other than that, they got to Tom's without a hitch.

Except Tom wasn't there, and James was just leaving.

"Hey," he smiled broadly. "You're just in time. Mum called from the hotel."

"Mum's in the hotel?" Amelia almost yelled.

"Where else would she be?" James looked at her, puzzled.

"We've got to get her out!"

"And my mum!" Charlie added. "And the guests."

James frowned. "Why would we do that?"

"Because there's a brood of alien spider babies in Bowler Hat Man's room and they've already eaten him up!"

To James's credit, he accepted their story immediately. Only weeks ago, he would have patted Amelia on the head and told her how cute it was that she still played make-believe with her friends. Now he didn't even ask her how she knew, he just went back to Tom's and opened the door.

Amelia and Charlie followed him inside.

"Whoa!" said Charlie.

Amelia stared. The chaos and clutter of Tom's cottage had undergone a radical change. James snatched up the phone and dialed the hotel, while Amelia gazed around her. Tom's messy piles of half-rolled charts and lists had been organized into five neat sets, and one whole portion of the desk had been cleared to make room for a huge square of grid paper. She could see James's careful handwriting in several different colors on the grid, and off to the side, scraps of paper with scribbled math equations, lots of crossing out, and several large, cross-looking question marks.

"Mum?" James sounded calm, but his expression was tense. "Amelia and Charlie are down here – they want you to evacuate the hotel."

He listened intently, then said, "I'll put her on," and held the phone out to Amelia.

"Mum, get out now!" Amelia said. "Charlie and I saw Bowler Hat Man go into the bush and dump a giant, empty spider egg sac, but it's not the real Bowler Hat Man, this guy is a fake. And now there are probably thousands of cannibal spider babies in his room, and they're going to eat everyone, and –"

"Amelia!" Mum was abrupt. "Stop!"

"But –"

"Amelia, I heard you and I'm taking you seriously. I'm so glad you told me straightaway. I'm going to tell Ms. Rosby as soon as I see her. Illegal alien immigration, visa overstay and invasion is her department, and she'll know exactly what we're dealing with."

"OK," Amelia said, "good, but you still have to get out!"

"Cookie, I can't evacuate the hotel on your hunch, *even*," she raised her voice over Amelia's protest, "even a very good hunch, which I know yours is. In our situation, with aliens we know little or nothing about, there may be more than one way to understand even the most suspicious behavior."

Amelia groaned.

"Anyway," Mum went on briskly. "Hadn't you better get a move on?"

"Why?"

"Oh, I thought James told you."

Amelia looked up at James. "Told me what?"

"Dad's with Control at Lady Naomi's. They're going to blow up the you-know-what."

On any other day, exploding an ancient alien spaceship would have been electrifying news, but right now Amelia's only feeling was relief that everyone who needed to know about the plague of giant spiders was together in one place. She slammed down the phone.

"What?" said Charlie.

"Let's go," said Amelia, already running for the door. "Lady Naomi's place – *now!*"

CHAPTER EIGHT

The three of them raced towards the clearing with the spaceship. James powered along easily on his giraffe legs. Amelia and Charlie kept up only by sheer force of will – there was no time to waste if Amelia was right about the alien egg sac.

Then, from the top of the hill beside them, someone else started running for Lady Naomi's clearing: the woman in the scarf. She streaked away from the hotel, cutting across the lawn in a frantic sprint that outpaced all of them.

"Look at that!" Charlie panted. "She's heading

for the spaceship too!"

"Maybe it's hers," said James.

Amelia didn't bother explaining how ridiculous that theory was. She just increased her pace another notch and moments later, crashed through the low-hanging banksia branch.

The woman in the scarf was already out of sight, but as the three of them leapt and ducked and swerved and twisted their way towards Lady Naomi's clearing, they could hear her. Oh, man, could they hear her.

She was screaming so loudly, her voice was sort of tearing in her throat. The thing that most shocked Amelia, though, was how frightened and heartbroken she sounded.

As they sped around the last bend in the path, Amelia saw Dad, Lady Naomi, and the Control crew all frozen in astonishment. Several long wires were already attached to the spaceship, buried in lumps of what Amelia guessed was plastic explosive. Or whatever aliens used instead.

"Please! Stop! You *can't*," the woman sobbed. She had fallen to her knees in the clearing and was almost lying with her face in the dirt, her arms stretched out in front of her, begging and abject.

Arxish stared down at her in disgust, then rounded on Dad. "Just exactly how many people know about this site and what we're doing here?"

When he saw Amelia, Charlie and James, his lip curled. "The children," he sneered. "I knew they would tell others. This whole facility will come under Gateway Control's direct authority when I've made my report, Walker. You'll be lucky to find a job scrubbing toilets after I'm done with you."

He was so boilingly furious, even Ms. Rosby looked nervous.

"Now, calm down," said Dad. "There's no need to –"

"*Don't* you tell me to calm down!" Arxish fumed. "You're the most incompetent, arrogant, ignorant –"

"All right," snapped Lady Naomi. "That's quite enough."

That made him stop. Arxish gaped in outrage. Amelia doubted he was interrupted very often. If ever.

"You dare to –" he spluttered.

"This is *my* facility," Lady Naomi went on calmly. "Gateway Control is here by my invitation, and so are the children."

Amelia felt so shy at this, she looked at her feet. No Grawk. She glanced over to the woman in the scarf, then back at James and over to Charlie. Finally she found a pair of luminous yellow eyes low in the grass as Grawk hunched in the shade of a rock. Who was Grawk hiding from?

Lady Naomi went on. "This woman followed me here the other day. It had nothing to do with the kids –"

That wasn't completely true, but Amelia was more grateful than ever.

"– and whatever her interest in the ship, I would like to hear her out before you destroy it."

"She lied to us!" said Charlie. "She said she was looking for her husband, but –"

"I am!" the woman cried, lifting her face again. It was filthy now, smeared with dirt and tears. "That's his ship! And he's still inside!"

"Nonsense!" Arxish scoffed. "The ship has been buried in the ground for almost seven thousand years, and we don't know how many centuries it drifted in space before that. Not even the Guild's deepest hibernation units could survive that long."

"And yet," Lady Naomi said evenly, "I still want to hear her story."

Arxish snorted and shook his head but before he

could speak, Ms. Rosby said, "Quite right. Come on, my dear, stand up now. You've got our attention."

Kindly, she shuffled over to the woman in the scarf and helped her to her feet. "Now then," she said, patting her arm and dusting some of the larger twigs off her clothes. "Go on."

The woman steadied herself. "My husband and I – we are among the last survivors of our race. Our people ..." She seemed uncomfortable, as though she desperately wanted to explain everything, but at the same time, felt desperately sure everything had to be kept secret. "The Munfeep," she said, and Ms. Rosby gasped, "are a very long-lived people, but we do not have many children, so there have never been many of us. We lived together quietly, in great prosperity and contentment, until the army of the Fourth Law decided to wipe us out and steal our homelands and all our wealth."

"The Fourth Law?" one of the Control agents choked out. "But that was ..."

Ms. Rosby looked at the Munfeep woman, her eyes shining. "That was twenty thousand years ago – nothing more than a myth to us now ..."

Amelia wondered what it must be like to be an old, old lady at six years old, and meet a woman who was still young after twenty *millennia*.

Arxish and the other Control guys shifted awkwardly. "My husband," she went on, "was on an exploratory mission, deep in the outer reaches of our galaxy when the Fourth Law found him. He sent me one last message, telling me he'd detected a rift in space, a kind of trans-spatial portal, that he could use to escape – this was long before the gateway system evolved, you understand – and that if he survived, he'd – he'd –" she sobbed, "he'd never stop looking for me."

She cried quietly to herself for a minute or

two, then raised her head again. "Since then, I've searched for him. It took centuries to narrow down even which galaxy that rift had connected to, centuries more scanning every sentient planet's transmissions for a clue that his ship had been discovered. And then, when I was almost beyond hoping, I read a notice from Earth to Gateway Control headquarters."

"You broke into our secure communications?" Arxish burst out. "You —"

Ms. Rosby quelled him with a single glare. "Go on, dear," she said soothingly.

"I knew at once it was his ship. I immediately booked myself on the next wormhole, and had just enough time to *reconstitute* myself."

"Reconstitute?" said Charlie. "What does —"

"But why didn't you tell us from the start?" said Amelia. "We could have helped you as soon as you arrived."

The woman didn't answer. Instead, she gazed at Arxish, his mouth hardened into a stiff, disapproving little line.

"The Fourth Law …" Arxish muttered, his face flashing with something halfway between disgust and terror. He quickly wiped the expression away. "Not completely unjustified …"

Amelia understood. Even without knowing a single thing about the Fourth Law, or the Munfeep, or whatever had gone on between the two, she could tell that Arxish saw this woman as a kind of grotesque fable come to life.

Luckily, Dad never noticed extremely awkward moments, so he plowed in happily. "Well, guys, I'm convinced! How about we deactivate the explosives and let the lady see her husband?"

"Of course we will," said Ms. Rosby. "Let's make it so."

Arxish couldn't slink away fast enough, almost

flinching as he passed the ship, now that he knew what was inside. So Dad disconnected the detonation wires.

The woman in the scarf walked over to the ship, hovering at chest height on its anti-grav field, and lovingly ran her hand over its surface. Amelia didn't know what there was to feel there, but after a second or two, the woman pressed her fingers into a small ridge and, with a soft hiss, the whole ship split in two. Immediately the first split divided into dozens of little splits, like branches off a tree. Suddenly Amelia realized that the ship was made of tightly fitting plates that were now moving and shifting, lifting up and sliding over one another so that an opening formed in the roof.

The woman stood on tiptoe, her face ablaze with happiness, and looked into the hole.

"No!" she whispered. "After all this time!"

"What's wrong?" said Lady Naomi.

The woman swung back, her whole body rigid. "It's empty!"

CHAPTER NINE

The woman in the scarf collapsed to the ground, like a balloon when all the air rushes out – only not at all funny. Ms. Rosby and Lady Naomi hurried to her while Dad, James and Arxish began discussing what might have happened to the man.

With the adults distracted, Charlie was free at last to go over to the ship. Amelia could see that it was too high for him to look inside, but she knew that wasn't going to stop him. He reached up to touch it. Instead of firm resistance, it spun on its anti-grav field, as easily as if it had been a log in water.

Amelia pushed aside her fears of alien radiation and joined him, watching as the open hatchway rotated towards them.

"Hey!" Charlie yelped. "Another one!"

Amelia's skin tingled all over. The inside of the ship *wasn't* empty. There was no alien inside, dead or alive, but there *was* some loose sand and, filling almost all the available space, another hollow, woolly bundle of webbing, just like the one the fake Bowler Hat Man had dumped in the bush.

The woman's head snapped up. "You've seen one of these before?"

"Yeah," said Charlie. "About twenty minutes ago. We were on our way to tell Amelia's dad about it."

"We phoned Mum," added Amelia.

"Where did you see it?" The woman reached

up to grip Charlie's wrist. He didn't look too happy about it, and Amelia didn't blame him. The woman was almost muddy with tears by now, her eyes swollen and her nose runny, and sitting in the dirt she looked pretty deranged. Charlie flinched, and she shuffled towards him on her knees. "Tell me! Please!"

Amelia was never so glad in her life that there were so many adults around, or that so many of them were Control agents and armed with explosives. If their theories were right, this woman's husband had somehow been eaten by the same spider alien that had eaten poor Bowler Hat Man.

"Tell us what it is," said Charlie stubbornly, "and we'll show you the other one."

As the woman hesitated, Amelia saw Arxish shudder.

The woman braced herself. "It's a cocoon.

Whenever my people are sick or injured or feel themselves getting too old, we spin a cocoon around ourselves and after a day or so, we emerge – reborn, almost. Our bodies are completely renewed, healed of any injuries or scars, and young again."

"Oh ..." said Charlie in wonder. "Not spiders – butterflies!"

"For thousands of years," she went on, "the Munfeep lived this way on our home planet, regenerating our bodies as needed. But then, K'Torl – my husband – discovered that by taking a little DNA from another species, we could reconstitute ourselves and emerge from our cocoons in a different body! Still ourselves – our own minds and memories and personalities, but in almost any type of body we liked. It was this, in fact, that set the Fourth Law against us in the first place."

Not even butterflies, Amelia thought. *More like fairy-tale genies – tricky, shape-shifting, and practically immortal.*

Arxish snorted, a harsh, judgmental sound, and for once Amelia didn't entirely blame him for feeling hostile. Not that she felt that way, but it was intimidating to realize how powerful the Munfeep might be.

"My husband should have been hibernating in his cocoon all this time," the woman said. "But how did he get out? His cocoon is torn open and empty, yet the ship was closed and encased in glass –" She stood up and turned to Charlie. "The other cocoon – will you show me now?"

"You bet," said Charlie, keeping his bargain.

"Don't worry about the cocoon!" Amelia said, almost laughing now that it was clear the hotel wasn't full of hungry alien spider babies. The real Bowler Hat Man was just fine after all. "We can take you to the Munfeep guy himself!"

"Who?" the woman said faintly.

"You had dinner in the same room on your first night here!" Charlie hooted.

"Look," said one of the Control guys, "can we blow this ship up or what?"

The woman didn't so much as glance at him, so fixed was she on Amelia and Charlie. She waved a hand over one shoulder and said, "Go ahead. The ship is nothing to me."

The woman nodded at Amelia, and began walking towards the hotel.

Amelia went to follow her. "Come on, Charlie," she called.

"You go. I'm good here, thanks."

"Charlie?"

He shrugged. "I'd rather see the spaceship explode. I've seen grown-ups meet old friends and talk about the old days loads of times already."

Amelia raised her eyebrows, but didn't argue. "Whatever," she murmured to herself. She had to jog a bit to catch up with the Munfeep woman, who hadn't paused at all.

As they got past the first bend and out of sight of Lady Naomi's clearing, Grawk slipped out from the undergrowth and joined her on the path.

"Is it the Control guys you don't like?" she smiled to him.

As they strode up the side of the hill to the hotel, Amelia said, "I can see why you would want to, ah ... reconstitute yourself as a human before you came through the gateway."

The Munfeep woman gave her a sideways look and said nothing.

"I mean," Amelia went on, "my mum freaked out when Bowler Hat Man didn't come out of his room for two days. I get why you'd want to avoid that. Plus, you'd have to dispose of the cocoon ..."

"Hmmm." The woman marched a bit more deliberately, and her face was stern. Amelia realized it wasn't an arrogant face at all, but *guarded*.

"I suppose you don't want to talk about it," she said at last. "Sorry."

The woman sighed, and then said, "It's not what I want or don't want – the Munfeep simply *do not talk about it*. After the Fourth Law killed more than half of us, and the rest of us scattered, we had to make ourselves invisible."

Amelia gasped. "You can do that?"

"No, I don't mean literally invisible. I mean, we melted into whichever world we found ourselves in – we hid away any clue that we were Munfeep, and as far as we could, we became identical to those around us. We have done it so well, most people have forgotten we ever existed. As you saw from those Control agents, a lot of people wish we never had."

118

"Oh." Amelia thought hard and walked on in silence.

As they got closer to the hotel, both of them sped up, skipping up the main steps to the front doors, striding across the lobby, and then almost sprinting up the marble staircase to the guest wing.

Amelia was slightly breathless as they jogged down the hall to Bowler Hat Man's door. "He's in that room."

"Right next door? The whole time?" The woman laughed softly.

Amelia wondered if she should leave and give them some privacy, but from the look on the woman's face, she'd as good as forgotten Amelia was there. All her attention was on the door to Room 7.

With a deep breath, she knocked. After a long pause, the door opened, and the new, younger, handsomer version of Bowler Hat Man stood in the doorway. He was still wearing his bowler hat, even in the privacy of his own room.

"Can I help you?" he said politely.

"Oh, I hope so," said the woman. "That is, if you don't mind, I need to ask just one question ..."

The man smiled quizzically. "Yes, all right."

The woman swallowed and then, looking him straight in the eye, spoke in a rushed, lilting jumble of sounds that Amelia guessed was Munfeep.

The man staggered back, his hand over his mouth. Then he replied in the same musical torrent, grinning. "Q'Proll?"

She gave a shout of laughter in return. "K'Torl?"

They talked hurriedly back and forth, and then suddenly the man threw off his bowler hat, and Q'Proll pulled her scarf back. Amelia saw, rising up from the hair on their heads, slender pairs of antennae. As Q'Proll and K'Torl stood nose to nose with one another, the antennae gently bobbed towards each other, and then entwined.

In that instant, Amelia knew two things: that Bowler Hat Man was, against all logic, the woman in the scarf's long lost husband, and that – as the antennae continued to wrap themselves into writhing knots – she was witnessing her first full-on alien kiss. It was definitely time to go and find Charlie.

CHAPTER TEN

The next day the snooty human woman, her two little kids and the quiet old lady checked out of the hotel, and no other human guest had made a reservation for the week.

Q'Proll and K'Torl asked if they could throw a party. Arxish looked a bit queasy at the thought of hanging out with a couple of Munfeep, but Ms. Rosby couldn't have been more delighted and accepted on behalf of Control. For a while, Amelia thought there might be an out-and-out argument between the two, but things calmed down when everyone realized just how lavish the Munfeep party was going to be. In fact, Arxish was so won over, he actually offered the use of his teleporter.

"How can you afford to pay for all this?" Charlie asked bluntly, gawking over yet another load of food, decorations and gifts that K'Torl had been busy ferrying back from Egypt with the help of the teleporter.

"I've worked most of the six and a half thousand years I've lived on Earth," he said. "I've saved a little here, made a few investments there ... it's amazing how it all adds up after a while."

In fact, when Charlie pressed him a bit harder, it turned out that K'Torl had accumulated *millions* of Egyptian pounds, as well as nearly four *billion* US dollars, several million British pounds, and similar amounts of Chinese yuan, Japanese yen, Euros, and Russian roubles, plus he owned some small islands in the Pacific Ocean.

"But they're not a long-term investment, obviously," he said modestly.

Charlie was speechless.

"Well, I got in on investment banking during the Middle Ages," K'Torl shrugged. "It wasn't hard to make a profit."

Amelia wondered what Callan would say if he knew ...

By lunchtime, the ballroom had been swept, dusted, aired out and mopped clean, and by nightfall it had been carpeted from wall to wall with gorgeous silk rugs. The walls had been hung with tapestries, and every table and chair was draped in the finest Egyptian linen. The tables were covered with gold-rimmed bowls and platters, and they in turn were filled with fragrant koshari rice, spicy meat, dozens of salads, sweet nut pastries dripping in rosewater and honey, fat dates stuffed with nougat and dipped in chocolate, and warm bread so soft and fresh from the oven it made you forget about everything else.

As if that weren't enough, K'Torl and Q'Proll had bought presents for everyone. Amelia still couldn't believe the lapis lazuli necklace they'd given her. Charlie, in a red fez, was overjoyed by the perfect creepiness of a real ancient cat mummy.

"Was this your cat, K'Torl?" he asked. "Did you mummify it yourself?"

"No," K'Torl laughed. "I'm more of a dog person."

James had finally put down his book of Ancient Egyptian astronomy charts and was dancing with Ms. Rosby, who had hooked over one elbow her new cane with the head of an ibis. Arxish and the two other Control agents had arrived so relaxed that, in violation of their own protocols, they had turned off their holo-emitters and were reclining on sofas like Cleopatras – if Cleopatra had been a twelve-legged land squid (Arxish), a thin, curly-furred monkey-rabbit, or a giant pill bug.

Q'Proll came and slipped her arm around K'Torl's waist – they hadn't been apart for more than three minutes all night.

"So what happened to you, anyway?" said Amelia. "How did you get out of your ship? That was like a magic trick!" Then she caught herself, and added, "That's if you don't mind me asking ..."

"No, it's quite a story," K'Torl said. He saw that Lady Naomi, Dad and Mum had drifted over to listen. Mary and Tom were too busy at the buffet table to care.

"Well," he went on, "as you already know, I crashed. The Fourth Law damaged my ship before I escaped through the rift, and I had little control over it as I shot out into this galaxy. I flew on for thirteen thousand years, until I was pulled into this solar system by your sun's gravity. I identified Earth as my only opportunity for survival, and managed to direct my ship into orbit. I was very weak at this point – I had been in hibernation for millennia, and though I had revived myself only a couple of decades earlier, I was out of food and badly hungry.

"When I crashed into the sands of Egypt, the impact knocked me unconscious and when I awoke, the entire ship was encased in glass."

"Buried alive!" Amelia said in horror.

"Indeed," said K'Torl. "But by my very good fortune, I was in the body of a Saurestian fire crab at the time, and it was very easy for me, even in that state, to crack the glass and dig my way out of the sand."

Amelia swallowed. *Crack the glass?* It had been

almost six inches thick in places! And digging through sand – how could he have survived?

"I realized that the glass was a great disguise for my vessel, and was able to emit enough heat from my claws to remelt the glass and seal up the pod again."

Charlie nodded. "Which is why it looked untouched when they found it."

"So there I was, on the surface of this alien world, a plume of smoke coming from the sand, and me all shaky with fatigue. Of course, I was soon surrounded by humans who had heard the crash. Poor creatures – imagine them there, trying to figure out what this big sign from the skies meant, and then seeing me crawling out of the ground in front of them. And as I was, all shining in my blue-and-gold exoskeleton, I looked like a giant scarab beetle. They thought I was a god. One poor fellow fainted of fright on the spot, while the rest ran away."

Amelia touched her necklace – a gold scarab beetle hung in the center between the blue stones. Perhaps for K'Torl it had brought back memories?

"I thought," he continued, "that they might have gone to fetch weapons, and honestly, I was so tired, I didn't care. I just lay in the sand and rested. But the dear things – it turned out they had arranged a sacrifice in my honor, and they brought me all sorts of meat and honey cakes and wine. Far more than any of them could afford, of course, but I didn't know that at the time. I just fell on it and ate it all. I'll always be profoundly grateful.

"Well, they were all around me, clapping and singing, and it was very kind and welcoming, but obviously it couldn't go on. Fortunately, I managed to snip a little hair from one of them – I believe he took it as a special blessing – and after I had eaten and rested enough to return to full strength,

I simply flew away to a more isolated place, and reconstituted myself into a human body."

"But you were all alone," said Lady Naomi, her face full of pity. She glanced over at Tom. "No one there for you, to help you survive."

K'Torl shrugged. "I am Munfeep," he said. "Being alone is how we survive."

"But you're not alone now!" Q'Proll chided, and snuggled closer into his side.

"Ah." K'Torl turned to her. "But I'm not just surviving anymore, am I? Now that we are together, finally I can begin to *live*."

Rolling his eyes and barely suppressing a gagging sound, Charlie dragged Amelia away.

"I wanted to hear what happened next!" Amelia protested.

"I already know what happens next," said Charlie. "The same thing that's been happening all night: they kiss and slobber all over each other for about an hour."

Looking back over her shoulder, Amelia saw that Charlie was right.

"But still," she said, "I wanted to know how he got here, to the hotel, at the exact moment that Q'Proll did."

"Oh, I can tell you that." Charlie threw himself down into an armchair.

"You can?" Amelia sat in the chair beside him.

"Yeah, he told Arxish he'd been hanging around the dig site since the archaeologists first found the ship. Like, a year ago or whatever. And then when Control's advance team went in a couple of weeks back, K'Torl overheard them talking about the gateway."

Amelia snorted. "You mean it was Arxish's own team that blabbed?"

"I know," Charlie grinned. "It's classic. Anyway, I've been thinking ..."

Amelia raised an eyebrow.

"It's about Q'Proll," he said. "She made herself human *before* she came through the gateway, right?"

"Yeah," Amelia said, not fully paying attention. "I asked her about that. I guess she felt safer getting it done before she left home."

"But where did she get the human DNA she needed?"

Now Amelia sat up straight. "You're right – where did she?"

"I've got a theory. Actually, I've got three."

Amelia nodded.

"One," said Charlie. "Someone like Leaf Man who comes here all the time could easily get a bit of human DNA and sell it to whoever was interested."

Whoever was interested? Amelia thought. Who would be? Apart from the Munfeep, who were so rare they had been thought to be extinct, who would want human DNA? And what would they do with it? Were there alien scientists out there somewhere doing experiments with human genes?

"Two," said Charlie, "there might be another human planet out there. Maybe because all life on Earth actually started somewhere else and just fell through the gateway accidentally back at the beginning of time, or maybe because that other planet started up a colony on Earth on purpose, or maybe there is just another planet out there with different DNA, but we kind of coincidentally look like the same species."

Amelia raised her eyebrows.

"It could happen," said Charlie. "Parallel evolution. Like with lemurs and squirrels – different species, but they turn out the same."

"I can tell the difference between a lemur and a squirrel," said Amelia.

"Whatever," Charlie said easily. "It's not my favorite theory anyway; I was just trying to cover all the possibilities. So now we're up to theory three." He leaned towards her. "I think that Earth is really the only planet with humans on it. But we're also the planet with the most active gateway in the universe. So what if someone from our side has gone through? What if there is a human being out there, somewhere, lost in the universe?"

All the hair stood up on the back of Amelia's neck. It was possible. Very possible. She remembered Tom warning them so angrily the first time Charlie had tried to sneak a look down the gateway stairwell – he'd told them how dangerous the gateway was, how the wormholes were always shifting and how things could accidentally get sucked through. That's how Grawk had ended up on Earth, after all.

Then she thought of the space on her wall

where that little locked safe door was, and the oil painting that used to hang over it – a portrait of Matilda Swervingthorpe, the original owner of the Gateway Hotel. She'd lived out here all alone ... right up until she'd gone missing without a trace.

"You're right," she said slowly. "I think that's exactly what's happened, Charlie. Someone, at least once, has gotten lost through the gateway."

"What's all this?" said a laughing voice. It was Lady Naomi coming over to them with a plate of fruit. "You're looking far too serious for a party."

Amelia and Charlie stared at each other. Someone getting lost through the gateway – and someone else spending all their time researching ... or was it just *searching?* What *was* Lady Naomi looking for with that equipment? Or *who?* And was she searching on Earth, or some other planet? What had she hoped to learn from that ship before they found out it was Munfeep?

Amelia's head spun with questions. Like, what did Q'Proll mean when she'd said K'Torl had gotten lost *before the gateway system evolved?* And now she came to think of it, with the gateway right there only a short walk from the hotel, why was Lady Naomi's research all being done in the bush in Forgotten Bay? How come she wasn't traveling to different parts of the universe through the wormholes whenever she wanted? And also –

"Amelia?" said Lady Naomi, a little concerned.

Amelia realized she'd been sitting there with her mouth hanging open, and shut it. "Sorry," she said quickly. "Just thinking."

"Thinking?" said Ms. Rosby, who was tottering by. "No time for that, my girl! Look over there – our dear Arxish has decided to give being Control's most pompous snob a rest for the night, and he's actually going to juggle for us. Come on –

it's the most dangerous sport on his home planet, and he's rather good at it. You must see!"

Amelia and Charlie turned, and there in a cleared space on the ballroom floor was one of Gateway Control's Big Three on Earth, standing on his huge squiddy head, and waving all twelve tentacles in the air, each one holding a knife, a sword, a full glass of wine, or an egg. Around him, the other Control agents, K'Torl, Q'Proll and the rest of Amelia and Charlie's families were standing in a wide circle. Ms. Rosby started a slow clap and the rest joined in. Some started to stamp the floor in time until the whole ballroom throbbed with the beat. And then Arxish started to juggle ...

Lady Naomi's face broke into a huge smile as she watched those flailing legs weave through the air faster and faster, Arxish's balance and timing impossibly good, not a single drop of wine spilt, and still he went faster. Every now and then,

one of the Control agents would give a shout of warning, and throw another object into the mix. There would be a little hitch and everyone would hold their breath, but then Arxish would get his rhythm back and keep juggling, now faster again.

It was just like the Gateway Hotel itself, Amelia realized. Every new piece of information they discovered brought another three questions up behind it. Each new part of the puzzle they solved just turned out to prove that the big picture was so much bigger than they had thought. She wondered if they would ever get to the end of it – if it would ever be possible to understand the gateway itself.

Lady Naomi gave a great whoop of delight and threw in a bunch of grapes. Arxish, driven on by the clapping and stamping around him, juggled faster again. And Amelia forgot all her wondering, and just enjoyed the crazy, impossible show.

Cerberus Jones

Cerberus Jones is the three-headed writing team made up of Chris Morphew, Rowan McAuley and David Harding.

Chris Morphew is *The Gateway's* story architect. Chris's experience writing adventures for *Zac Power* and heart-stopping twists for *The Phoenix Files* makes him the perfect man for the job!

Rowan McAuley is the team's chief writer. Before joining Cerberus Jones, Rowan wrote some of the most memorable stories and characters in the best-selling *Go Girl!* series.

David Harding's job is editing and continuity. He is also the man behind *Robert Irwin's Dinosaur Hunter* series, as well as several *RSPCA Animal Tales* titles.